KISSES FROM PARIS

AMBER GHE

HUSTLE & WRITE PUBLISHING

To my daughter's
Briandi Bryant, and La'Ryn Allen
I love you.

KISSES FROM PARIS

CHAPTER
ONE

KANE

"So?"

"What?" I asked. Aspen's question reminding me that she was still on the phone. "Now you know they don't invite the kids who were in special ed. to the class reunions."

"Give me a break. You're in Paris to become a Master Sommelier. That's like having a double PH. D. in wine," Aspen blew out. "Most of the people in our class aren't half as successful as you are today, and they didn't have—"

"I know," I answered immediately. My uncertainty made my voice harsh and demanding. "I'm sorry. But I'm honestly not interested in going to the class reunion at Montbello High School. Thanks for thinking of me, but I really need to focus," I softened my voice before reaching up to adjust the earbud sitting in my ear.

"I didn't mean to make you uncomfortable Kane. I can't help but admire the fact that you decided to further your education in wine."

I think she knew she'd gone too far.

"How long will you be studying abroad? It would be amazing if I could come visit." Aspen questioned.

"You should definitely come for a visit. It will probably be a year before I'm comfortable enough to take the exam. The exam is very extensive. Most don't pass on their first try. There's a reason why there are only two hundred and sixty-nine Master Sommeliers worldwide, twenty-eight of them are women, and only three are black," I pointed out.

"Wow, no, that sounds pressing."

She was right, it was pressing, and I wasn't sure why I was putting myself through the trauma.

"I want this so bad," I spoke eagerly. "Speaking of bad, young lady. Let me remind you to stay out of trouble while I'm gone," we laughed.

"You don't have to remind me. I've had enough woes for a lifetime. I'm on the straight and narrow now. But you're over in Paris, the land of love. You might just find a big, tall tree while you over there," Aspen laughed.

"Girl, you are too much, and while that sounds ideal, I'm much too busy to entertain your foolishness," I shook my head. There was no room for romance with my busy schedule.

"Kane, I cannot wait until you get back. You and I branching off as partners to open a wine club is going to be epic," Aspen stated.

"This is going to be exciting. I'm so ready for this next chapter in our lives." I lifted my arm to look at my wristwatch. "Ooh, I gotta get off here. My shift is starting," I noted.

"Okay, girl, call me later. Love you."

"Love you too. Bye." I ended the call, pulled my earbuds out of my ears, and dropped them in the pocket of my trousers along with my wine key.

Inside, Andrew, the other sommelier, and I received updates from the previous team. They handed us the 86-list, which referenced no longer available wines, allowing us to remove those items from the wine list before service. Andrew and I headed into the kitchen.

"Hey Fred," I said.

"Kane, Andrew, how are you today?" Fred, the chef on our shift, asked.

"Good," Andrew and I stated in unison.

"Beautiful. Well, today, our special is roasted salmon with sorrel sauce and lemon," Fred told us.

"Thank you," I answered.

Andrew and I moved on to our station to clean, uncase, and restock items they sold from the last shift.

"How was your weekend?" Andrew asked as we worked diligently to get everything stocked promptly.

"It was decent. I finally got some much-needed rest. What about you?" I asked as I picked up the 86-list and struggled to read its contents.

"Emily and I took the kids to the park and

had a picnic. It was nice to relax and spend time with the family."

"That sounds wonderful," I said, opting to spray out the ice buckets instead.

"Well, we're open for service," he noted. "We better get busy."

"Yeah, it's my turn to take supplies down to the cellar. We can switch after the first hour," I told him.

"Okay, sounds good." Andrew headed out into the restaurant. I picked up a box of wine we didn't need and headed down to the cellar. Andrew was a nice guy, and like me, he had immersed himself into the French culture for a year. Life doesn't get much better than when you get to study abroad. You get that combination of architecture, culture, food and also learn from a great mix of people from all over the world. Andrew, his wife, and kids came from Spain. I admired the way he fought to become a master sommelier.

Down in the basement, I put the box of wine we wouldn't need away, grabbed a box of our more popular dinner wines, and headed back upstairs to restock. I picked up several of the wine filters that I thought we would need during our service and laid them out.

Halfway through the service, Andrew came out and said he had an emergency phone call he needed to take and asked me to cover for him.

"Table six is where I left off," he said before heading outside to take his phone call. I grabbed a couple of wine menus and headed out to table six.

God, he was beautiful. Then our eyes met.

"Shit," he said.

The intrusion of that word he spoke pulled me out of my head.

"I just got this suit out of the cleaners," the fine ass man said.

Boy, he was even finer up close and personal.

"What an idiot," the woman he was dining with blurted out.

My embarrassment turned to raw fury at her words. He held his hand up to hush her.

I quickly grabbed the towel draped over my arm and dabbed at the liquid I spilled on him.

"I'm so sorry," I apologized as I hurriedly

attempted to wipe the water away before it could soak into his clothes.

"Don't worry about it," he offered in a voice that wasn't as condescending as I expected it to be.

"If you need to return the suit to the cleaners, please send me a bill," I offered. As I tried my best to stop staring at his package that was so obviously not affected by the cold water I'd spilled on his lap.

"I can probably get your bill discounted as well."

I was completely mortified as he grinned at me. I looked away to avoid his gorgeous smile. However, I couldn't stop my gaze from returning to that damn bulge in his slacks. I reasoned it was only to assess the damage I caused.

He looked at my badge. "Kane, huh?" His eyebrows shot up. I knew he was observing my name, so he could complain to my manager.

"Yeah," I shook my head.

"I'm Seven," he extended a hand.

I wiped my hands on my apron so that I could shake his.

"That's a nice name," I breathed.

"Thank you. Do you think I could place an order?"

I cleared my throat. "Oh yes, your order. What would you like?"

Seven sat the towel down on the table. "I really like the profile of a Barolo from Italy. Do you have something from a nearby region?" He asked.

"We don't have a Barolo from Italy, but I could offer you a Barbaresco, the same Nebbiolo grape but from a different region," I said. "Or would you prefer a different grape same region?" Despite my nerves, I forced myself to settle down.

"What do you recommend?" He asked.

"Well, if you order the house special this evening, I would suggest white wine, something that leaves a hint of sweetness on the tip of your tongue, and maybe a bit of oak? However, if you're going to have steak, I could suggest a great red wine for you," I explained.

"Thanks for the suggestion. I'm definitely in the mood for ribeye steak."

"May I suggest a Cabernet Sauvignon something from the Robert Mondavi reserve?"

"Yes, that sounds excellent," he noted.

"Great. The waiter will be over to take your dinner orders while I get your wine," I said, rolling my eyes at the blonde-haired woman he was dining with. I was actually trembling now. Too bad he was dating an asshole.

Still, I collected the wine menus and headed back to the kitchen area.

CHAPTER
TWO

SEVEN

Remembering the ice-cold water hitting me in prohibited places caused a slight smile to grace my lips when I noticed Kane and I were in the same class.

Pay attention. I told myself. The master sommelier test was a beast. That's why there was only a handful of us there in the first place.

Kane was a gorgeous woman. I found that she kept drawing my attention. However: now that the teacher was talking and things were moving in class, I used the teacher as a focal point.

"So even though we will meet once a week, Master of Wine is a self-study program, a journey you will embark on, on your own. With that being said, I'm going to place you in study groups. Do not fail your team. Show up and put in the hard work. Now I am going to count off every four people. Whatever number you count off is the group you will be with."

After the teacher counted off the groups, everyone went to their respective corner of the classroom. To my surprise, I ended up in the group with Kane. *How was I supposed to focus with that beautiful woman as my study partner?*

"Hey, I'm Seven Smith. I'm from Napa Valley, California," I introduced myself to the rest of what would become my study team.

"Hi, my name is Kane Amore. I'm from Colorado," she said.

"Hello, my name is Bill, and I'm from Iowa. This is my second time attempting the test."

"Hi guys, my name is Kelley. I'm already acquainted with a few of you, and I'm from California. It's nice to meet you guys."

"California in the house," I joked. I noticed Kane rolled her eyes. "Yeah, my family has a bookstore in Napa Valley, but I'm here because I aspire to own a vineyard one day," I noted, trying to keep tensions at bay.

"Cool," Bill replied. When will everybody be ready to study, and how do you guys want to meet?" He asked.

"Well, maybe we could meet at the restaurant because we'll need the wine to practice," Kane added.

"Yeah, that's true," I replied.

"Bill, you said you took the test before? That's great because you have a little insight into how things will go," Kane pointed out.

"Yeah, that is a plus," Bill added.

"If everyone is available, we can get started after class," I suggested, and everyone agreed.

After class, I took off in a slight jog to catch up with Kane, who was already walking toward the restaurant.

"Hi, do you mind if I walk with you?" I asked.

She looked around me. "Where's your girlfriend? Shouldn't you be walking with her?"

"Kelley is not my girlfriend. We were studying yesterday."

Kane smirked.

"I'm really sorry she acted that way. But you have skills. I peeped your wine game," I smiled at Kane.

She smiled. All the annoyance on her face softened. "Thanks, I appreciate that. So, your family owns a bookstore, but you want to own a vineyard?"

I nodded. "Yeah, I do. It's ironic that you asked me that because my older brother is going to take over the family bookstore. I'm thankful because that doesn't interest me at all. It's not that I don't like books, I love to read. But wine is my passion."

She revealed open admiration at my words. "That's exciting," Kane said.

"It really is. I've been planning this thing out for years. I know an older gentleman who's waiting on me to buy his vineyard. What brings you to Paris?" I inquired.

"My friend and I are going to open a wine bar in Las Vegas. Hey, you could be our supplier," she joked.

"Hell yeah, the Dom, the King Pin. I'm

gonna make you an offer you can't refuse." We laughed at the movie reference to The Godfather. I turned around to walk backward so I could face Kane. "I'm serious."

She squinted. "I'm serious, too," she replied, her mouth curved into an unconscious smile.

We entered the restaurant and spotted Bill sitting at a table by the window. He waved at us, and we headed his way.

"I ordered a sandwich. I was starving," Bill told us.

"I'm going to order something, too if we're going to be drinking," Kane said.

"Good idea," I noted, picking up the menu.

Moments later, Kelley joined us, and it seemed as if Kane's demeanor changed immediately. I nudged her. "You good?"

"Yeah," she nodded. Still, a frown fell into her features.

"Hey, guys, let me establish this before we get started. We are all here for the same reason, and none of us is better than the next person. Let's agree to be respectful of each other because we'll have to spend a lot of time together before we take this test." Everyone nodded in agreement.

We started on the flight of wine the sommelier brought out to us.

"How would you describe this?" Bill asked.

Kane sniffed the wine before tasting it. "Dry and tantalizing," Kane answered.

"Citrus and tropical fruit notes," Kelley added.

"I taste green apple and tangerine notes," I said, swishing the liquid around in my mouth.

"It's vibrant and crisp. It's Chardonnay," Bill answered. "Is that what everyone guessed?"

"Yes," me and Kelley answered collectively.

"Oh, dang," Kane said. "I guessed Pinot Grigio."

"It's easy to confuse the two," Bill noted.

We went through another round of questions, and Kane missed the answer again. Kelley high-fived Bill.

"We got this, Bill. We're going to ace that test," Kelley bragged.

Kane's eyes darkened.

"You guys have a good day," Kane remarked, gathering her things. "I have some things to do."

Kelley was working my nerves, and I knew I needed to squash this shit.

CHAPTER
THREE

KANE

When I got home, I kicked off my shoes and sat on the edge of the couch to rub my aching temples. I'd been excited beyond belief to take this class. Now, I was so over this already. Kelley caused an inner torment to gnaw at me. I was trying to remain professional, but I really wanted to show her who Kane from the 'Bellows' was. *Focus, get your certification so you can go on with your life.* I told myself.

After I got myself together, I took a shower, grabbed some microwave popcorn and a glass of wine, and climbed into bed.

The first thing I did was pick up my cell phone to call Aspen.

"Aspen, you must've jinxed me when you started talking about the big, tall trees because I served this guy yesterday. He was so fine, but girl, why did I spill water all over his lap?"

"Oh my god, no, you didn't," Aspen laughed.

"Yes, I did. I was so embarrassed until the woman he was with called me an idiot."

"Oh, hell no, girl. Do I need to book a flight?" Aspen spat.

"No, because I don't want to get kicked out of this program. But you already know," I smirked. "As for the guy, he wasn't mad. He seemed really nice. I showed off my knowledge of wine, making a great suggestion to him."

"Did you get his number?" She asked.

"No, I went on about my business, not giving him a second thought." I fluffed my pillow behind my back. "So, check this out. Today I go to class, and they're both there. We all ended up in the same study group," I growled.

"Oh, my goodness," Aspen said. "Is he dating that girl?"

"Well, we talked a bit today, and he said he wasn't. But it's important to establish a baseline since we'll be study partners. Aspen, you know that I fought too hard to get here to let it go downhill over some big, tall tree," I joked.

Aspen laughed. "But hey, it's nice to know there are some cute guys over there. I hope you guys hit it off," Aspen said.

"Really, you're just going to disregard what I said? I mean, yeah, if we could exchange numbers for the future, that would be cool. But I don't have time for anything right now, and that kind of sucks."

"Yeah, I know what you mean, but do you know how fast the time will go?" Aspen noted.

"I guess you're right. Anyway, girl, I love you. I'm going to rest my mind for a bit, eat this popcorn, drink a glass of wine, and get some rest because I work at the restaurant tomorrow."

"Okay, I'll talk to you this weekend. Love you."

"Love you, too." I ended the call and sat

the cell phone down, took a sip of wine, and threw my head back.

The next day, I got up and took advantage of an open schedule and got study time in over a cup of coffee. I looked at my watch. It was time for work. I grabbed my backpack and coffee and headed that way.

The lunch crew was already in full swing when I arrived. I noticed Seven, Bill and Kelley already posted up studying. My heart sank because as much as I liked Seven as a study partner, I didn't care for Kelley at all. I didn't like her negative vibes.

I headed back into the kitchen to my workstation.

"Hi, Andrew."

"Hey, Kane," Andrew greeted. "You know you got the first shift today?" He reminded.

"Yeah," I answered. I really wanted to trade with him to avoid my study group, but I sucked it up and headed out to take orders.

I headed over to their table.

"Hey, guys, what can I get you?" I asked.

"Hi Kane. Can you get us a flight of wine

and surprise us with the selections?" Bill asked.

"Yeah, I can do that," I noted.

"Too bad you have to work while we get to drink wine," Kelley smirked.

"Oh, I don't have to work. This is my study time. Hands-on experience, you know?" I grinned.

"Seven," I breathed and then cleared my throat. "Um... hi."

I avoided his eyes, but I could feel them on me. I pulled my lip into my mouth.

"None of us exchanged numbers with you yesterday, so we weren't able to tell you we were meeting today," Seven said.

"I could give it to you now," I replied. He handed me his cell phone, so I could type in the information.

I gave him a slow glance over and tucked my hair behind my ear.

"You know I can call you later and update you with my notes," Seven offered.

"Sure, that'll be nice. I'm only here until 4:00 p.m. today," I added.

"You two aren't flirting, are you?" Kelley asked, giving off a dry chuckle.

Without a response from either of us, Kelley breezed off to the restroom.

When I got off work, I said goodbye to Andrew and headed outside.

"Kane."

My throat constricted when I noticed Seven waiting outside. "Seven, what are you doing here?" I asked.

"Well, I thought I'd give you a ride instead of calling you when you got off. I thought maybe we could chat in person."

I shrugged. "I guess we can," I commented, as my hands nervously moved to straighten my clothes.

"I'm parked right over there," he pointed.

I followed Seven to his car, and he opened the door for me.

"Thank you."

"You know we could go for a ride. I'm sure you could use a few moments to wind down since you've been working," he said once he'd gotten in on the other side.

"Sure. You know what? I haven't had any time to check out the scenery here, so that would be nice." I relaxed into the plush leather seat and realized I was tired from being on my feet all day. We were quiet, but it was nice just being in our thoughts.

"You know, Seven, you're really a nice guy, but I don't think I'm going to work with the study group any longer. I'm not feeling Kelley, if you know what I mean." I didn't want him to pity me. I only wanted peace to do what I had to accomplish my goals.

"I know she can be a pain, and I'm sorry. I wish there was something I could do. I tried to ask everyone to be respectful of each other, but she doesn't take a hint, does she?"

"Some people are just like that. But I'm going through a lot, and I know I need to buckle down. I fear she's going to throw out one of her little comments, and she's going to make me show her who I am. I really don't want to do that."

Seven let out a loud chuckle. "No, we don't want that. We've worked too hard to be here in the first place."

CHAPTER
FOUR

SEVEN

Kane was the type of woman men coveted. The sculpture of a woman always took my breath away.

"You know, I realized our study sessions didn't go well, and it's even crossed my mind to say forget it and go back home." Kane sighed.

I was just getting to know Kane, so I opted not to respond right away, fearing I'd push her away. I definitely didn't want her to leave.

We went to Champ De Mars, the public park in Paris near the Eiffel Tower, and sat on one of the benches. People were having picnics and riding their bikes down the pathway.

"It's beautiful here, isn't it?" Kane commented.

I nodded. "You know I was thinking about what you said about leaving. I know we're just getting to know each other but still, it's killing me that you were struggling with the study group the other day."

Kane's insecurities flashed across her eyes. "But I could be your tutor if you gave me the opportunity. I even got one up on that. Let's make a pact that we'll both stay, take, and pass the test. What do you say?"

She shook her head. "How will you tutor me when you're in a study group with two other people? You know the teacher said not to let each other down," Kane replied.

"Yeah, that's true; however, the teacher doesn't know that you're being bullied by one of the students, and instead of complaining about it, we're just gonna do our own thing," I told her.

"You would really do that for me?" I heard her breath catch.

"Hell yeah, I want you to get this," I

licked my lips. That must've tickled her because she kind of swatted at me.

What do you say we walk over to that little café and get a bite to eat?"

"I say it sounds like a good idea." Once we were seated inside the café, we ordered French pastries and coffee.

"These are so good. My dad used to work at a French restaurant when I was in middle school, bringing home big boxes of pastries every day. They were so good. That's what this reminds me of," Kane's eyes closed as she reminisced.

"Sounds like good memories. Do you have other siblings?" I inquired.

"I have a younger sister. She's in college now. What about you?"

"Well, I think I mentioned before that I have an older brother. His name is Rye."

"I swear you guys have some nice names. Your mother must be very unique," she said, her fingertips spread across the mug she was holding.

"I think my mom's secret passion was to be an author. She never quite did it, so owning a bookstore was like the next best thing. I'm sure we got our names from some characters she read about in a book. I don't know?" I shrugged, and Kane smiled.

"That is so cool and interesting. My parents split up when I was young, but they always remained cordial with each other. We still did things as a family, so if it was one of our birthdays, our parents still got together and threw us a party." Her features became more animated. "Sometimes, we all had dinner as a family. It was like they got along better when they weren't around each other every day," she said.

"Yeah, I get it. That's a good dynamic. I've never known anyone whose parents were split up and still had a good experience behind it," I noted. I took a bite of my pastry and then sipped my coffee.

"Yeah, that's one thing I always enjoyed about my parents." Light rekindled in her as she thought about them.

"So, Kane, you never told me whether you agree to the pact? Are you going to make a pact to stay, to study? Are you going to let me help you?" I asked.

"Seven, there's something that I need to disclose before I can make a pact with you."

"Okay, I'm listening," I said, curious since the look on her face had changed.

"I have a learning disorder, dyslexia." She kept her head down. "When I was in fourth grade, I had a teacher who called me an idiot and said I should've studied harder when I failed the test."

Kane closed her eyes and shook her head before speaking again.

"So, when Kelley called me an idiot the other day, it brought up a bunch of feelings that caused me to feel insecure about everything. We both know this is a very hard test. I'm already a sommelier. I mean, I'm lightweight, wondering if I even wanna put myself through all the scrutiny," she said.

"I understand what you're saying. I don't know much about dyslexia, but I'm willing to help you. I mean, obviously, if you're a sommelier, you know your stuff. You can become a double expert. I believe in you." I held my fist out for Kane to fist bump with me, confirming the pact, and she did.

"We got this," I confirmed.

"Yes, we got this," she repeated. From here on out, we're going to work super hard," she said.

I prayed I didn't fail her.

The next day, I showed up at Kane's a little before time. I wanted her to know I was about my business. With two bottles of wine tucked under my arm, I rang the doorbell. My phone chimed as she opened the door. It was Rye, telling me to call him, which I would do later. Right now, I had tunnel vision on getting Kane and myself to a comfortable place to take the exam.

"Hi," she lifted her eyes to mine as I entered the room.

"Hey. I brought wine for us to study," I said. Kane grabbed the bottles and sat them down on the table.

"Let me get glasses," she said, leaving the room.

Even her silhouette was breathtaking. I stood there looking around. "This is a nice place."

"Thanks," she said, entering the room. "It'll work for the time being."

"How are you?" She chirped as she got busy setting up a laptop and the glasses.

She'd also brought in a spit bowl for each of us.

I stood there, looking at her, realizing she made my stomach churn with excitement.

"I printed up some checklists for us to work through," she tucked her hair behind her ear again.

Shaking my head, I moved towards the table to have a seat. She joined me.

"I hope you don't mind. I have software that reads to me. It makes it easier for me to study.

I nodded. "I understand. Feel free to utilize me as well."

"Right, I forgot," she said.

"I figured today we could talk about the three A's, acidity, aging, and aeration," I explained. I couldn't lie. She looked good as fuck when she picked up the glass and dipped her tongue into the contents. It was going to be a long evening.

CHAPTER
FIVE

KANE

I sighed. "This is confusing." We'd spent the last few hours working through the three A's and the notes of the two wines we had to work from. He smiled at me, clearly trying to ease my anxiety about the situation.

I shrugged and crossed my legs. "I don't know if this is worth it," I sighed.

"Come on with it, stop playing. You know this," Seven crooned.

I took him in. Adidas fitted tee showcasing the muscles in his upper body, and matching sweats showcasing the print I tried so hard not to notice.

I waited to be sure he was done before I

answered. "Full-bodied Cabernet Savion?" I asked. Seven's lips curved, giving me the indication that I'd answered correctly.

My lips spread into a full grin.

"I told you I had your back," he declared, making me giggle.

"I know I've thrown a lot at you, so we can call it a day if you'd like," Seven admitted. "Hopefully, I didn't go too hard on you?"

I nodded as he pushed back from the table.

"Should I come to your house tomorrow?" I asked.

"I say we stay here where you're most comfortable," he assured.

"Thanks, that sounds good."

"What ya doing?" I said to Aspen on the phone.

"Your ears must've been ringing, girl. I have a customer right now who wants some wine/weed pairings for a party. Tell me that part again," Aspen begged.

I rolled my eyes. "Girl, if you don't write this stuff down."

"Thanks, because who knew you could pair wine with weed?" Aspen giggled. "I have a pen and pad. Go ahead. I'm ready."

"Okay, I'm going to repeat this one more time. Merlot and Blueberry go well together. Rosé and Strawberry Cough go together, and then you pair Riesling with OG Kush. That's all I have right now."

"That's enough to get her started," she said.

I sucked my teeth.

"Hold on," Aspen said.

My brow wrinkled as I listened to her wrap things up with the customer. I picked up the wine glasses and headed to the kitchen.

Aspen came back to the phone. "Thanks. You made a sista look good. Like I know what I'm talking about to a certain extent, but you take it over the top."

I turned on the water and began to fill the dish tub in my sink with hot soapy water.

"So, what's up? Did you ever see the guy that was in your class again?" Aspen asked.

I smirked. "We're study buddies. We made a pact to see this thing through together."

"Shut the fuck up."

"Don't make this awkward, Aspen. We're study buddies. Key word study," I said.

"Let's see. Paris, plus wine, plus a big tall tree equals romance."

We laughed.

"Your math sucks. I told you I'm on a mission, and so is he. End of story."

"Yeah, okay. You either need a man or some herb to smooth out your edges. That's why you've been so uptight."

"You might be right, but instead, I'm going to bed. Love you," I told her.

"Love you, too."

After finishing up in the kitchen, I grabbed a glass of wine that I would actually drink and headed out to the terrace. The Eiffel Tower was lit and a gorgeous sight to see from my vantage point.

Aspen was right. Maybe I was uptight because I needed a man. Hell, my last boyfriend didn't know how to talk to people, and I was fed up. But Seven seemed so generous and compassionate. I mean, this man was taking time out of his day to ensure I studied and succeeded at this test. His personality was sexy all by itself. The fact that he was good-looking was icing on the cake.

The next day was a class day, and I was running late. I managed to shower and pull myself together in record time. I slipped in quietly as the professor lectured on storing and serving methods.

My eyes went to Seven who smiled at me. He was so damn sexy I could barely concentrate during the lecture.

"Hey, beautiful," Seven complimented.

I blushed. "Hi."

"I know I said we could study at your place today, but I was actually hoping for a change of scenery."

"I'm down for whatever."

"That's what I like about you. You're spontaneous, not to mention your green eyes are gorgeous." Seven pulled his lip in when he said that. Making me spill satin in my panties. Lord, it was probably a good idea to go somewhere neutral.

CHAPTER
SIX

SEVEN

"Oh my God. This might be my new favorite spot. This is delicious." Kane stuck another bite of food in her mouth.

"I thought you might like it. I was starving, so I knew you had to be hungry as well." She nodded. I was happy she seemed to be warming up to me.

"I know we need to study, but I was hoping I could confide in you?"

"Is everything alright?" Kane's brows pressed together in concern.

"Well, the other day, when I was coming to your house to study, I received a phone call from my brother. I didn't answer since we were getting ready to study. I figured I would give him a call later." I paused, unable to speak. "Well, come to find out, he's in the hospital with stage four cancer."

"Oh, my goodness, Seven. What can I do to help?"

At that moment, I wanted to be deep in her womanhood. I wanted to be with a woman who cared about me like this.

"I don't know," I shrugged. I knew in my heart I needed to get home to see my brother, but how was I going to do that when I made a pact with Kane about the test? This was about to be bad.

We sat in silence for a few moments. Kane reached across the table and placed her hand on top of mine. Honestly, the human interaction meant so much to me.

"It's okay. The way you said you were here for me, I'm here for you. I got your back," she said.

I lifted her hand and kissed the inside of her wrist. I never had a woman tell me that she had my back. My ex-girl-friend, Kimberlee, was a pain in the ass for real. Everything was always about her. If anything in this world happened, she found a way to turn it into a situation about herself. Not sure what I ever saw in her.

"Do you want to talk about it?" She asked.

Kane was so down to earth. She was a gorgeous and modest woman. That, to me, made her even more intriguing.

"I need to go home. I don't know what that's going to mean for you and me and our study plan." I sucked in angst before speaking again. "I feel so horrible because I was trying to help you, and I put my foot in my mouth. I'm a man that's used to fixing shit, but I can't fix this."

Kane blew out an audible breath. "I understand. You might not be able to fix the situation, but I'm sure your brother would probably just want you there. This might be the confirmation I needed to go home," Kane admitted.

I shook my head no. "That's not gonna work. We've just got to figure this out."

"That means a lot to me, but your situation is more pressing," she said.

I snapped my finger. "How about you go home with me?"

"Me? You want me to go home with you?" Kane asked, looking perplexed.

"Yeah, why not? I mean, we can continue our studies on the plane and when we get home except for when I'm visiting my brother. I just fear that something will happen if I don't get home. I need to see him."

"Well, I think as long as they give me time off at the restaurant, it shouldn't be a problem. I could maybe meet up with Aspen while we're there. That's my best friend, the one who lives in Las Vegas," she explained.

I massaged the five o'clock stubble on my chin and wrapped my hand around my tense neck. "That would be perfect," I nodded.

"We can go back to my place to make the arrangements and book the tickets," she suggested.

When we got back to Kane's place, she opened the door, and I followed her inside. But once we shut the door, I had the sudden urge to kiss her. I backed her up against the door and put my mouth on hers. She didn't resist, so I kept going.

"I'm sorry, it's just that being around you feels good," I whispered in between kisses. But I shouldn't have spoken because that kind of broke the momentum.

"We better book these tickets," she reminded me.

"Yeah, you're right."

We sat down at the table while she began plugging away at the numbers to book the flights.

"Give me the airport you use," she inquired.

"It's Oakland," I replied. "We also need to rent a car because it's still a fifty-mile drive from there."

She shook her head. I was trying hard to hold it together. I knew she sensed it because she stopped what she was doing and grabbed my hand, pulling me up from the chair. I wrapped my arms around her as she sank into my chest. I desperately needed that hug. I scrubbed my face, not wanting her to see the emotion infiltrating it.

I pulled back. "We should finish."

"It's done. Come on," Kane pulled me to the couch.

I cleared my throat. "Thank you," I attempted to re-compose myself, but her perky nipples sat at attention. It was distracting.

"No, studying today." She said. "Sit."

I sat down. It was like a boulder lifted off my shoulders. I leaned back.

"You know how a lot of siblings fight all the time? Well, that wasn't my brother and me. In fact, we were always very close and did everything together. I can count on one hand the number of times we fought with each other," I shook my head. "But he used to hold grudges with other people a lot, and I would tell him let that shit go, Rye. You're going to make yourself sick. It's literally not good to hold grudges in life with anybody. He's a good guy. He just never learned how to release the negative. I was the opposite. I wasn't going to let anything or anyone rain on my parade. I would brush my shoulder off and keep it moving with the quickness." I paused at the lump in my throat.

"That's so crazy that you brought that up. My grandpa used to tell my sister and me that exact thing that being mad would invite disease into your life." Kane sighed as she laid her head on my chest.

"You know I never thought about being in this world without my brother."

"Stop, don't do that to yourself. People have medical miracles all the time," she said.

"Yeah, and like I said, I'm always the positive one, but he's already planning for the worst. I hate to admit this, but this could derail my entire plan to open the vineyard because I'd have to help my parents with the bookstore."

"I just think you're putting the cart before the horse. Stop trying to foresee the future."

"Yeah, you're right. Ugh. I hate feeling like this. It's so not me to be down in the dumps," I sighed.

"I believe you. I met the person who offered to help me through my woes," she smiled.

I squeezed her hand. Her head on my chest and hand in mine felt natural.

"Have I ever told you, you were sexy?"

CHAPTER
SEVEN

KANE

I bit my lip and met his gaze.

"You think I'm sexy?" I asked.

A smirk climbed his face. "Hell yeah, you're sexy," Seven licked his lips. His mood and energy suddenly felt really good. He laid me back on the couch. I surprised myself with my willingness to comply, despite the nervous energy that danced inside me.

Fuck it. Aspen was onto something when she said I needed some 'D.' His mouth dropped to mine. He wasted no time reaching under my skirt and planting a hand on my inner thigh. The bulge in his sweats caused me to gasp.

Seven's cologne filled the air as we kissed. I felt the intensity of his affection as it spread through each of my senses. But I could also feel the resounding hurt in him. The lines on his forehead revealed worry.

"I'm sorry," he said. "I want you, but I'm burdened with concern for my brother right now."

I palmed the sides of his face. "I understand you're emotional right now and don't know how to channel it. That's understandable."

We were convoluted in emotion. I put my eyes on him to soothe him as I straightened my clothes.

I admired the complexity of this man. I knew we had a connection, and I desperately wanted to fix his broken pieces.

The next day, we sat on our flight together, holding hands.

"Kane, I want to thank you so much for supporting me in going home. It really means a lot," Seven stated.

"No, thank you. You were the first one to step up when I needed help and support, so I'm just returning the favor."

I laid my head back. We didn't get much rest making last-minute plans and packing. Thankfully we made our flight on time. I prayed everything would be okay with Seven's brother.

We both took naps before they came around with our meals. After we ate, we studied just like he said we would. I was thankful because I really needed to keep the information at the forefront of my mind. I needed to live, eat, and breathe wine until I passed that test.

Several hours later, when we landed in Oakland, we grabbed our rental car and took the drive to Napa Valley.

During the ride, we continued to study as much as we could, discussing wine and the different aspects of storage, the type of glasses that you use for different occasions, and anything that we could study without actually having a glass of wine in front of us. And I was messing up. I didn't understand what was going on because I knew this stuff, but for some reason, it wasn't working out. It wasn't coming to me as it should.

"This is useless," I said, slapping my hands down on my legs. "I'm not even sure why I agreed to this. I should've gone home when I had the first thought to do so," I told him.

"Kane, I really can't do this right now. I know you're stressed, but I need to get through seeing my brother first. I will make sure that I get you together," Seven blew out.

"I'm so sorry. I didn't mean to be selfish." I said, dropping my gaze.

Seven lifted my chin. "It's alright."

"I know that you're going through a lot right now. I'm literally scared. I don't understand why I'm putting myself through this misery."

"You have to trust that you were called to do this for some reason. You were called to show other people who have dyslexia that they can learn, and can overcome a learning disability. It may take a little more time. You may have to take that test more than once, but you can overcome. Don't let it get you down," He encouraged.

I pulled my lip in in an attempt to keep myself from tearing up. I really didn't mean to be selfish during this time when he needed to see what was going on with his brother. A test could be taken at any time, but for his brother, that was something that was unknown. It wasn't known whether he would wake up the next day or not, so I really needed to get my thoughts in check. I nodded in compliance.

This was my first time seeing Napa Valley. It was fascinating to see all of the vineyards along the roads, so many vines and varieties of grapes. It was beautiful. I snapped photos along the way and sent them to Aspen. Once we got to Seven's town, we went straight to the hospital. His parents were already there. They came down to the parking lot to greet us.

I released the air in my lungs I'd been unknowingly holding as Seven stood off to the side to greet his parents. His mother seemed really happy and excited for him to be home. Then he motioned for me to come over. I couldn't explain the knot in my stomach as he introduced me to his parents.

"Mom, Dad, I'd like you to meet my girlfriend, Kane. She's also in Paris studying to become a master sommelier."

"Hi," I gave a short wave to his parents stunned Seven introduced me as his girlfriend.

"Hi honey, it's nice to meet you. So glad you were able to come with my son. I'm sorry that it couldn't be on better terms," his mother expressed.

"I'm sorry, too. I pray everything will be alright," I told his mother as she squeezed my hands.

"Thank you," she said.

"It's so nice to meet you," his father said, shaking my hand.

"Nice to meet you," I answered.

"She came with me because we're studying. We studied on the plane ride, and during downtime. We're going to continue to study while we're here. Both of you know that the exam is extremely hard, so we need to stay on top of this thing."

"That's wonderful," his mom said. "We're actually going to run and get some lunch. You two go on up and see Rye. I'm sure he'll be excited to see you. We'll bring back some burgers and fries for everybody," His mother told us.

"That would be great. I'm starving," I said, rubbing my belly.

CHAPTER
EIGHT

SEVEN

We watched as my parents climbed into their truck and drove away.

"Don't you wanna go inside?" Kane asked.

"Yeah, but I'm honestly not prepared for what I might see. I'm a little unnerved by all of this right now."

"Come on. I got you," she told me.

I looked into her eyes, and she gave me a look assuring me that she, in fact, had my back.

Kane grabbed my hand and pulled slightly until I followed her into the hospital. We stepped into the elevator, and she gave me another one of those soothing hugs that I needed. I pressed my lips to her neck.

I couldn't believe I had introduced this woman as my girlfriend to my parents. It was my first time bringing someone home to meet my parents as an adult. I hadn't brought a girlfriend home since Kimberlee.

I glanced at Kane. She was so freaking gorgeous. I was proud to have her on my arm. I couldn't wait for my brother to meet her. We stepped out of the elevator and headed up to the information desk. I asked about my brother, and they pointed us to his room. When we reached his room, I tapped on the door.

"Rye, it's me, Seven. Are you decent? I got my girl with me?"

"Seven? Yeah, man, come on in," Rye said.

We stepped into the room. I was still nervous until I saw him. My brother honestly looked like he was in good shape. I was surprised. I didn't know what I expected. I went straight over to him, gave him a big hug, and then we slapped hands.

"Yo man, you look good. How are you feeling? You look like you will be getting out of here sometime soon?" I asked

"I don't know, man. My prognosis isn't good, but I'm just trying to do my best. Who is this?" His brother asked.

"Rye, this is my girlfriend, Kane. I met her in Paris. She's also studying to be a master sommelier."

"Hi, it's nice to meet you," Kane said, doing her little wave thing that she does when she meets someone.

"Kane, it's nice to meet you. Too bad you met this boy first. I can assure you if you met me first, you'd be my girlfriend," he laughed.

"Man, are you crazy? You always tried to take my ladies," Seven laughed.

"Have a seat, stay and visit for a minute," his brother said. We sat down in the brown armchairs they had in the room.

"Okay, let me tell you. This boy here always had a nice-looking lady on his arm. None of them have been as nice looking as you, though," Rye laughed.

"Oh, my goodness. So, he was a lady's man, huh?" Kane asked.

"Kane, don't even listen to him. He's over here starting some stuff," Seven joked.

"Man, you remember that time when it was snowing outside, and we had climbed up on the roof? Mom kept telling us to stop going up there, but we were hardheaded. We just loved to climb. We didn't usually have cold winters, but that one particular time, we had a little ice," Rye laughed.

Seven doubled over with laughter.

"Yeah, and then mom came outside and was calling our names? We stayed really quiet. I'm surprised she didn't see us there. We were barely hanging on." Kane had joined in on the laughter.

"We had so many good times together," Rye reminisced.

"We will have many more," I assured him. I noticed when I said that, the smile immediately dropped from my brother's face.

"Man, I don't know. They're telling me that they won't be able to fix this, that I'm too far along," Rye sighed.

"Don't go off what those people say. It's what's in your heart. You got to believe that you're gonna get better in your heart," I said, trying to pick my brother's spirits up.

"Yeah, he's right, you know. I know someone who was diagnosed with cancer. He went to another country for a healing retreat.

He was healed when he came back. They called it a medical miracle," Kane said.

"Hey, do you think you could get that information now?" I asked.

"Sure, all I gotta do is call my friend. She'll get the information for me." Kane stepped out of the room to make a phone call.

"I'm so glad to see you, though, bro. How is it over in Paris?" Rye asked. "It must be nice. You done came home with a whole honey dip on your arm," he joked.

"I can't lie. It's nice over there. I'm doing what I can, studying and drinking plenty of wine." I smiled.

We sat there for a minute, looking at the TV. Our parents came back with bags of hamburgers and fries for everybody. Kane followed them in.

"I got that information for you," she said.

"Rye, I got you a burger and fries. I don't know if you're up to eating, but it might make you feel better if you eat something," mom said. "I'll make that soup you like this weekend."

"I actually have a little bit of an appetite

today, so yeah, I'm ready to eat something," he told mom.

I glanced over at Kane, who was getting along with my family exceptionally well. I noticed her and mom having a separate conversation about books. I knew that was mom's thing. She was in heaven talking to someone about books because she usually couldn't get that from us guys. Kane looked my way. I winked at her, and she smiled. I couldn't lie. I was falling for her.

Later that evening, after we left the hospital, I took Kane by the vineyard I was looking to purchase.

"I know it's dilapidated because old man James was unable to keep up with the harvest. I just pray I'm able to get it before anything happens to him."

We walked through some of the rows of grapevines. "You know this place is actually amazing," Kane said. "You could breathe life back into it. We could even come up with our own line of wines. I mean, I can visualize the whole thing."

"Come here," I said, holding my hand out for her and pulling her in for a hug. "You are the most amazing woman I've ever met. I like how you included 'our' when you mentioned creating a line of wines."

"Oh, you caught that, huh?" Kane slipped her hands underneath my shirt.

We kissed. "Don't start anything you can't finish out here in these vines."

CHAPTER NINE

KANE

Seven dropped his mouth to mine and slipped his tongue inside. It was the type of kiss that would make any woman swoon. I was pleased when he slid his hand underneath my skirt and slid my panties to the side.

"Mmmmn, we can't do this now. Where is old man James?" I whimpered as he slowly pressed his thumb to my clit. He moved to work his fingers between my legs, finding a very swollen and deprived clit. I almost lost my shit when he sank two fingers inside me.

"He doesn't come outside after dusk. I tried to warn you when you slipped your hands under my shirt, touching my sensitive spot and shit," he gave me a sexy smirk.

I pulled my lip in and unbuckled his pants. I grabbed his dick using the pre-cum to slide and twist my hands around it.

"Fuckkk," he grunted as our gaze met.

He caught my leg, draping it over his arm for easy access.

"Shit," I whimpered as he pushed into me, filling me up. I held onto his shirt, fearing I would lose my balance on one leg.

"Don't worry, I got you," he whispered. "I needed to feel you."

Seven plunged faster and harder as I held on for dear life.

"Seven," I panted until we hit our peaks, and he let my leg down. I buried my face in his chest, and he wrapped his arms around me as I gained my composure. "Baby," I said. "I don't think I can walk."

Seven threw his head back and laughed before picking me up and carrying me back to the rental car. I sat in the car, reeling from what we'd just done and making sure my clothes were on properly.

We went back to his parent's home. Seven led me straight to his bedroom. Again,

I unbuckled Seven's belt in record time, pulling his dick out before he had time to blink.

"Damn," he growled.

The intensity of my mouth and the pressure of my tongue around him caused Seven to close his eyes. He reached for my neck, guiding me to his spot as I wrapped my full lips around his shaft. So much tension, he tried to hold back, but the sucking and me taking him down my throat caused him to release. Licking him clean, Seven met my gaze. He pulled me up and lifted my T-shirt over my head, exposing my hardened nipples. We kissed, and I knew this was my life. He laid me back on the bed, guiding me to spread my legs wide for him.

I squirmed as he lapped and teased his way to my breast. I groaned as his mouth pulled and tugged at my nipples.

I was slightly embarrassed when he moved down, face between my legs.

"Oh, we're still going to study," He said. "Mmmn, sweet, fruity, and floral notes."

Now that tickled me. But then I was right back into it when Seven sucked and blew on my clit, holding me steady.

"So, fucking good," I mumbled.

He dipped into me.

"Please," I whined, rocking my hips. He slid in and out of my liquid warmth until he couldn't stop. Making it his mission to make me cum as hard as he could.

Then he pulled me to the edge and pushed his dick inside me full throttle. He rocked me back and forth until we came into rhythm with each other. His hands and mouth were still working my breast. I never felt so connected with any man in that way. It was like our souls were intertwining with each other with every stroke. He played and dipped and circled inside me until I couldn't take anymore. My whole lower half shook, and then he moved faster until we were both on the quest to bliss.

He lay on top of me, breathing hard, our bodies still connected. We lay there passed out in each other's arms taking a short nap.

After the amazing dinner his mother cooked, we studied into the wee hours of the night. But for me, it was the stolen glances and lip pulls that kept me interested in studying. This man could be talking about donkey shit, and it would be interesting. He was so charismatic and entertaining when it came to tutoring me in a way that helped me understand on a different level.

In bed, we were both exhausted. I relished in the fact that he held me tight all night. The next day we prepared to go into town. Seven was going to visit his brother and I was going to have lunch with Aspen, who had flown in to spend the day with me.

I dropped Seven off at the hospital and programmed the GPS to take me to the area where restaurants and shopping were prominent. Inside the restaurant, Aspen was already seated, waiting on me.

"Aspen," I sang, as we gave the double cheek kisses like they do in Paris.

Hey, you look great," Aspen mused.

"Don't look at me like that," I laughed.

"You know what I'm gonna say? You look like you've been, you know, self-medicating," she laughed.

"Don't be telling all my business," I told her, shaking my head. "Yes," I shifted my gaze away from her, confirming what she suspected.

"Kane, that's great."

"Yeah, I guess," I let out a deep breath. "The only thing is we've been getting so friendly that I'm having difficulty concentrating when we actually study."

"I'm sure you'll be prepared," Aspen added.

"I appreciate that, but I'm telling you this because we're friends," I pushed out a sigh. "But meeting Seven has really thrown a boomerang in my plans and has me even thinking differently about my future."

"I don't understand what you mean."

"I mean, I don't know if I can go on with this test."

"I honestly think you're putting way too much fear into something that already comes naturally to you," Aspen said.

"You know, I never thought about it like that. Wine does come naturally to me. Sometimes even though I want to give up, I feel like Seven has put so much time into making this work that it would be bad of me to back out, especially now." My eyes were glued to Aspen for acknowledgment.

"Anyway, I don't wanna dampen our time together, but Seven has been so amazing to me, so thoughtful. He's catering to my every need. His family is amazing. Everything just feels so right."

"Girl, you know what I went through with Power, so I definitely understand your woes. I also understand what it feels like when that new love hits," Aspen smiled.

"I feel so alive. I want the discomfort of thinking about the test to go away. I want to enjoy the new love that I found."

"Yes, of course. I know it's your decision, but you're going to take the test if I have to drag your stubborn ass there myself," Aspen grabbed my hands. "Stop stressing."

We ordered a light lunch and continued talking.

"So, check this out," I said. "Seven took me by a vineyard yesterday that he's looking to purchase."

Aspen hiked an eyebrow. "Really?"

"Yes, I was playing at first when I suggested him becoming our supplier, but it only makes sense. Also, girl, I even had thoughts about starting our own line of wines."

Aspen shook her head. "Mmmmn, now you got my wheels spinning."

"Exactly, the possibilities are endless."

Aspen and I finished lunch, then went out for a walk through the town. We did some window shopping, stopping at the boutiques.

"Thanks for getting that information for me for Seven's brother," I said.

"No problem. I hope he uses it," she said.

"Yeah, me, too. Hey, here's a bookstore. Let's go inside and take a look around," I suggested.

Once inside, I realized it was Seven's mother behind the counter.

"Kane? I thought that looked like you," Mrs. Smith said.

"Oh, hi, I completely forgot. Seven told me you guys had a family bookstore. This is gorgeous," I said, looking around. "This is my friend, Aspen. She flew in overnight from Las Vegas to spend some time with me today."

"Hello, it's so nice to meet you, Aspen. If you ladies love romance books, I just got a new shipment in today. Come over here, and I'll show you where I'm setting them up on a new display."

We followed Seven's mom over to the display. Immediately Aspen squealed seeing some of her favorite authors.

"Nothing for you, Kane?" His mother inquired.

"I love books, but I actually do audiobooks," I told her. I looked over at Aspen, who could sense my apprehension.

"Audiobooks are good, but honey, there is nothing like holding a good old book in your hands," Mrs. Smith acknowledged.

I hated that this was going to be how I told her I had a learning disability. "You know, Mrs. Smith. I don't know if Seven told you, but I have dyslexia. I have a hard time reading. Sometimes the words just look like a huge clump, and it's hard to distinguish the letters. Some days are better than others, but if I want to enjoy a good book, I do audiobooks."

"Oh, my goodness, I'm so sorry, honey. It never crossed my mind. Sometimes we forget to be mindful that people may have things that they're dealing with," Seven's mom said.

"It's alright. I'm used to it," I added.

"No, it's not okay. It's not something that you deal with on a day-to-day basis. Thank you so much for pointing that out to me. You know you have inspired me to carry audio-books in the future," Mrs. Smith added.

"That's great," I smiled.

Mrs. Smith placed her hand on my shoulder. Now I know you're taking a difficult exam, so I'm extremely proud of the fact that despite your dyslexia, you're trying to become a master sommelier just like my son. That's amazing. You're inspiring to other young girls with learning disabilities," she said.

"You know, I never thought of it like that," I noted.

"Well, I keep trying to tell Kane that she's amazing. She has a great spirit," Aspen chimed.

"Thank you, guys, so much. I greatly appreciate you."

"Well, Aspen, come on over here honey with your books, and I will get you rang up."

CHAPTER
TEN

SEVEN

My brother looked great and was in great spirits. My parents were making arrangements for him to go to the healing retreat. I was excited that my mother was going to accompany him there. So, with everything going in a positive direction, we headed back to Paris.

We opted to go back so that we could spend some time studying without the distractions of traveling. We knew there was a sample test coming up that would give us an indication of how we needed to get ready for the big test. On the plane, we studied. And when we got tired, we laced our fingers together and took a nap. Once we landed at home, we studied hard for the upcoming exam.

"Are you ready for this, babe?" I asked.

"Yeah, you know I talked to your mom. She was telling me how I would be an inspiration to other people who have dyslexia. That gave me confidence, so I feel pretty good right now," Kane admitted.

"That's great. I'm excited to see how this is going to play out."

"Me, too. We should stop and get a pastry and coffee before we go to class, so we're not distracted and hungry while we're testing." Kane suggested.

"Yeah, that's a great idea. I have a bit of a headache this morning, so I think the caffeine will help."

"Oh no, I hope you're alright?" She asked.

"I'm good. It's nothing a little coffee won't knock out."

I parked the vehicle, and we ran inside. We knew we didn't have much time, so we got our stuff to go. We ate in the car. By the time we pulled up to the University, we were finished with our pastries and took our coffee inside.

The professor was headed to the front of the room when we sat down.

Bile built in the back of my throat at the thought of taking the exam.

"I hope you guys enjoyed your break. Now we are going to get back into the swing of things. I decided this would be a good time to take the practice exam midway through the course, giving you time to brush up on the areas that you may need to work on," the professor said. "There are three sections of this exam - taste, theory, and practical service. I want everyone with their original group. I do realize that some of you have split up. However, for testing purposes, I want everyone with their original group. Group one in the cafeteria for taste. Group two, please head to the auditorium for theory, and groups three and four will stay here for practical service. Thank you."

We spent a good portion of the day going through each exam. I'm not going to lie. It was stressful, making for a long day. I could feel the tension in my shoulders, so I couldn't imagine what Kane felt like. Yet, she seemed to be holding up well.

At the end of the day, the teacher gave us our results.

"Oh my God, I passed!" Kane squealed.

"That's great, babe," I said, pulling her in for a hug.

I opened up my packet to see my results. "I didn't pass." I shrugged. *Wondering what I did wrong?* "I actually wasn't that far off," I said.

"You know it's probably the added stress being worried about your brother and everything," Kane noted.

"Yeah, not to mention the headache that I was fighting all day," I added.

"I'm thankful that this was a practice exam, so you still have time. We'll keep working hard. We don't want to forget anything before the big exam," she stated.

I gave Kane another big hug. "I'm so proud of you, baby. I told you I had your back."

She smiled. "You're amazing. You knew exactly how to get me to learn this stuff. I know Ms. Kelley is bewildered right now because she didn't pass after acting like an ass to me. I'm not going to gloat, though, because that's not my style. I'm just thankful right now," she said.

"As you should be," Seven said.

We headed to the car and got inside.

"How's your headache?" I asked. "Want to go to the park to relax for a bit? I would love to get some sunshine after that stressful morning," Kane suggested.

"I feel better. Sounds good." We went back to the park and sat on our favorite bench. It was nice taking in the fresh air, the sunshine, the butterflies, and the birds. It was very serene and peaceful. Then my phone rang.

"Hello, Mother, how are you?" I greeted.

"Seven, Rye is gone!" Mom wailed into the phone.

"Mom, what are you saying? Did he leave for the resort without you?" I asked, hoping I misunderstood what she was trying to tell me. I tried to change the scenario in my mind to fit what I was hoping she wasn't telling me.

"No, he'd only been home a couple of days. We thought he was getting better. But this morning, I went to check on him. He was dead. Seven, Rye is gone," I dropped my phone in my lap and cried.

"Seven, what's wrong?" Kane asked, draping herself over my back. I moved my mouth to say what had happened, but I couldn't get my voice to come up. My lips moved, but the words were stuck in my throat like a lump.

"He never made it to the resort, Kane." My words choked me, causing me to pause. "I had a feeling that if he got there, they would heal him, but he never made it."

Kane threw her hand over her mouth. "Oh, no, Seven. I'm so sorry."

"Rye kept talking to me like he was leaving, but I tried to keep him in good spirits. He was telling me that I had to step in and help mom with the bookstore. That the money I wanted to use for my vineyard was gonna have to go towards some renovations and expansion in the bookstore." The sting of the tears in my eyes was embarrassing.

"I told him I wasn't interested in that. I wanted to open my vineyard. Why did I tell him that?" I questioned, swiping my face.

I found my place in Kane's arms as she rubbed my distressed shoulders.

"You know, this wine thing isn't my plight. It's time for me to go home and make sure my parents are okay. Take over the family business so they can retire." I broke our embrace. "I don't understand because I saw him. He looked good. He was eating. He was getting better."

"I'm so sorry. You don't have to think about that right now give yourself some time." Kane cried.

I shook my head. "I told you I had your back, and you passed. You got this, baby girl, but now it's time for me to go back and do what I gotta do for my family."

We sat there for what seemed like a couple of hours. I wasn't in any condition to drive. I didn't even want to leave her side because I knew once I left, there was no turning back. I didn't know what that meant for us. We were just getting to a point where this thing felt good. All of our stars were lining up. But like I said, two things happened to me - not passing the test, and my brother passing was all the validation I needed that I was headed in the wrong direction.

CHAPTER
ELEVEN

KANE

Seven wasn't in any condition to be alone last night, so he stayed at my place. I held him all night as tight as I could. I wanted to show him I had his back, but honestly, this whole thing was terrible.

My stomach hollowed at the fact that Seven would move on without me. I knew he had to go back home to his life, and I would be going back to mine. That would be the end of this thing that we started. For now, though, I would hold on as long as I could.

It was morning. Seven seemed lighter after a hot shower, breakfast, and coffee. I put on my uniform, grabbed my bag, and kissed him.

"I can ask if I can have another day off. My boss has been very gracious in giving me time off, you know?" I told him.

"No, I have some stuff I gotta do today anyway. Thank you for being here for me, though," Seven said.

He stood up from the kitchen table and pushed his chair back. He walked over to me, pulling me into a warm embrace. "I know we haven't had much of a discussion. I just have so much on my mind right now," he said.

"No, I understand. Don't worry about it right now." I said. He reached for my hands. I held my breath.

Moments later, I broke away, opening the front door. We both stepped outside. It was a drab-looking day.

"Kane."

I turned to him.

"Can I give you a ride?" Seven asked.

"No, I need the fresh air. I feel like walking, but I'll call you later, okay?" I waved.

Seven nodded, moving towards his vehicle. I headed over to the restaurant.

When I got to work, Andrew was happy to see me.

"Hey, girl. I'm glad you came back," he smiled.

"Thanks, I'm glad to be back."

"How was your trip?"

"It was great. I got to visit a vineyard. I met up with my old friend from high school and had a nice time," I answered opting not to put Seven's personal business out there.

"Wow," sounds like you had a great time," Andrew said as he set the glasses out for the wine.

"How's the family?" I asked

"Oh, Emily and the girls are doing great. I heard you guys had a practice test over at the university?" Andrew inquired.

"Yes, and guess who passed with flying colors? Heck, if I didn't have to have so much experience under my belt, I would go on and take the test now."

"Unfortunately, that part sucks, especially if you know you can pass the test right now."

"I hope it wasn't a fluke, that I really know my stuff."

"No, I don't think you can fluke that test," he nodded.

We went on about our day working and serving wine. When I got home that evening, I hadn't heard from Seven causing fear to sink into my bones. Yet, I didn't want to worry him. Instead, I kicked off my shoes, tossing my bag onto the couch.

I picked up my phone and called Aspen, needing to vent. "Hey girl, how are you?" I asked.

"I was wondering when you were going to call me. What happened on that practice test?" She asked.

"Girl, you are never going to believe that I passed that test," I said in some weird voice before laughing.

"No way, see, and you were so worried," Aspen shrieked.

"I know. I can't believe it."

"Sounds like you should be celebrating, right?" Aspen asked.

"Listen, we were basically sitting in the park relaxing after the test, trying to just come down from the commotion of the day, when Seven's mother called. Girl, his brother passed away. He never even made it to the resort," I explained.

"Oh my God. I'm so sorry to hear that. Is Seven alright?" Aspen asked.

"He seemed to be taking it pretty rough. I mean, he's thankful that he went home. He got to see, talk and laugh with his brother. But that's the part that is so confusing. I swear he looked good. Rye looked like he was getting better. He didn't look like somebody who was on their deathbed for real."

"You know, some people get a second wind, or it's kind of like a false high where they look like they are doing good. They're energetic. They make plans, and then they just pass on," Aspen sighed.

"You know, I've heard of that happening. It's aweful. I'm just really sad about this. He's going to go back to his hometown to take over the family bookstore so his parents can retire. Like that's the end of the whole vineyard thing that he was dreaming about. That we were dreaming about that together." I stood up to pace the room.

"I'm so sorry to hear that, but you know where there's a will, there's a way," Aspen said.

"When he didn't do as well on the test, Seven used his brother's passing away as confirmation that he's supposed to go home. He's giving up on everything. I don't know what to do."

"Don't give up on him. I'm praying for you. I know it's getting late there, so I'm gonna get off of here. Plus, a couple of customers just walked through the door."

"Yeah, I understand. I'll call you tomorrow. Love you," I said.

"I love you, too."

When I hung up, I called Seven. He didn't answer.

"Hey, I'm off. I wanted to check on you." I left a message on his voice mail. Then I shot a text. *Hi babe, how are you?*

I showered and stalled around mindlessly watching TV, hoping to hear from Seven when I finally found sleep.

CHAPTER
TWELVE

SEVEN

I felt bad I had ignored Kane's phone call and text the night before. I looked at my phone. There was yet another message asking if I was okay. So, I got myself together and headed over to her house.

Stopping on the porch to admire the Eiffel tower in the backdrop, it was crazy how things could change so drastically. How I went from visualizing my life the way I wanted to to now, not knowing who I was.

I tapped on the door. I knew Kane wasn't expecting me because she was lounging in an oversize T-shirt, her hair was pulled up in a high bun when she opened it. She stood in the door frame holding a cup of coffee.

"Hey," I greeted her with a hug after taking a second to admire her natural beauty. She pulled the door open for me to step inside. I closed the door behind me as my feet ventured over the threshold.

"You had me worried since you ignored me all evening."

I drew her into my embrace, and she melted. "I'm fine. Just a lot of stuff on my mind. Kane leaned back to look at me. I gripped the sides of her face before peppering kisses on her forehead. I spent the day with her acting like a couple; a couple that would never be.

I felt like straight dog shit for what I was getting ready to do, but I slid out of bed when Kane was in a deep, peaceful sleep. I headed into the other room and grabbed a pen and paper, where I wrote her a note.

I threw my jeans and T-shirt on and grabbed my sneakers. I headed out the front door, ensuring to lock up behind me. On the porch, I put my tennis shoes on before moving toward my car. When I got home, I jumped on the computer to purchase a plane ticket.

I showered, packed, and left. It was early morning as I headed over to the airport to catch a flight home for my brother's memorial. I went through all the formalities of getting the rental car once I got to Oakland. Then I drove home. With every mile, I felt sickened at the way I left Kane without saying goodbye to her face.

At home, I pushed myself to move up the stairs to my mother's house. She burst through the door, hugging me so tight. We cried together.

"Seven, I can't believe he's gone," Mom said.

"I know, Mom. I know, but he's not in pain any longer. You have to remember that part," I consoled.

"Come on in the house, hun," dad said. "You're going to make yourself sick again." Dad picked up my suitcase and headed inside. I guided mom inside as well.

"We'll have the memorial tomorrow. Then Friday, we'll have the reading of Rye's will. You know we don't want to hold you up too long from school." My eyebrows wrinkled in trepidation.

"Mom, don't say that. Of course, I'm supposed to be here. Rye was my best friend." Besides, I don't even know if I'm going back."

"Why? You're so close to finishing. And what about Kane?" Mom questioned.

I shrugged. "I don't know Mom like I really am falling for her, but my priority is here right now with my family," I added.

"I'm sure she'll understand," Mom patted me on my leg.

I stood up and grabbed the afghan blanket that was sitting on the couch. I laid it over mom's lap and propped a pillow behind her.

"You relax. I'll make you some green tea."

"Thank you so much, son. I love you."

"I love you, too," I replied.

I never did hear from Kane. I suspected she took what I said in the letter pretty hard. I didn't bother contacting her, either. I didn't know what to say. I felt like a coward. I was letting her down. I didn't have her back.

I got in my rental car and rode over to the vineyard, walking around checking out this year's harvest. It was Wednesday, so I knew Mr. James was gone to Bible study. I was super sad that this place wasn't gonna be mine, especially after I had come here for years and manifested, so to speak, that this place would be mine.

When I arrived home, I noticed we had received flower arrangements. I looked at the names. One of them was from Kane to my mother, and another one was from Aspen, also addressed to my mother. That was nice of them. There was food for days where the neighbors had fried chicken, baked pies, cakes, and everything.

The next day we had my brother's memorial. It was the hardest thing I ever had to do in my life, laying my brother to rest. I spoke at his service.

"You know, Rye. You always had to outdo me. You always had to be the best at football, the best at basketball, the best at everything, so I don't understand why you couldn't be the best at staying here in this lifetime. Why did you have to leave me? I questioned, but I know you're not in pain any longer. I know that's the best for you. I tried to tell you to let go of all that anguish. I'm telling everyone who is here today, don't hold grudges. Be at peace with yourself."

I stood there contemplating my words. I stepped down from the podium. My dad stood up to hug me.

Soon after that, we left the cemetery heading back home.

"You know, Seven, I'm not really up for the reading of the will, so if you don't mind, I'm going to postpone that for a while," Mom noted.

"No, ma'am, that's completely under-standable. I'm not in a rush to do anything," I told her.

"I also want something else. I want you to go back to school and get that master sommelier certificate."

"But Mom, Rye wanted me to take over the family bookstore. If I do that, I don't need the certification."

"Trust me on this. I'm asking you to go back to Paris and get that certification. Then we'll talk about it," she said.

"Is that why you're not going to do the reading of the will? Do you already know what it says? Are you scared that I'm not gonna follow through with my dreams?"

"I just know that you've already put too much time into that to back down now. So, if you want to make me happy, remember, we are in the land of the living. Take your own advice, because if you don't, you're going to live your life bitter and broken. I want you to go back and get that certificate."

CHAPTER
THIRTEEN

KANE

I was so hurt to find that Seven was gone. When I rolled over, I didn't think too much of it at first—thinking that maybe he went out for coffee or something. So, I got up, showered, and started my day. It wasn't until I went into the living room that I noticed a note on the table—a real live Dear John letter.

I thought that kind of stuff only happened in the movies. I picked up the letter and read.

Dear Kane. I'm sorry that I am leaving without telling you face to face. I'm going home to my brother's service. At this point, I don't know what's going to happen. I'm not sure I'll be back. I know you'll do well on the exam, but if I don't make it back, I want you to know that the time I spent with you was amazing. You are a beautiful person. You deserve a good life. I'm telling you now if I have to run the family book-store, I won't be able to provide the kind of life you deserve. But keep your head up, baby girl. I love you. Seven.

Wow, so the very first time that he tells me he loves me is in a letter where he's breaking up with me.

I got up and went about my day. I was stoic. I had no emotion. I almost questioned why I didn't just get on a plane and go home my damn self.

God, why had you allowed a man to drop in my life suddenly only to leave as suddenly as he came? It's just not fair. I've always gotten the short end of the stick. I have dyslexia. I've always been left out and bullied. I came all the way here to be a master somme-lier, only to be bullied as an adult. Then I found the one thing that makes me happy, and now he's gone.

I was lovesick. I needed this to end. When I got off work, I grabbed a glass of wine, and headed out to the terrace. I wanted to call Aspen, but then again, I didn't. I was embarrassed to tell her what was going on, so I sat there looking at the moon, thinking about life in general, when my phone rang.

"Hey Kane, what you been up to?" It was my baby sister, Liz.

"Hey girl, how are you?" I asked.

"I'm good. I was just wondering why I haven't heard from you in a while." She asked

"I'm sorry. You know I have been out here struggling to study, trying to make sure I pass this test, and just living life. How are you doing? How is college treating you?" I asked.

"I'm doing all the typical college stuff, you know, trying to get in the sorority, study-ing, and doing a little bit of partying," she laughed.

"I remember those days. Are you good?" I asked, knowing my baby sister never called. She wasn't a phone person. This new genera-tion was all about texting.

"Yeah, I had it on my heart to call you. I wanted to make sure you were okay. I needed to put a little bug in your ear that I love you.

I'm so proud of you. I know it's hard, but I think you should keep going. See this thing through, Sis."

"Wow, thank you so much. I needed to hear that. I wish the same to you, Sis. "Keep going," I told her.

"I will. Well, I love you. Call me soon," Liz said.

"All right, I will. I love you, too. Thanks again for calling." I ended the call. It's funny how when you almost thought you were at rock bottom, there was always somebody lying in wait to remind you to keep pushing.

The next day was a class day. My heart sank when I noticed Seven wasn't there. I don't know what I expected because I knew he was gone. I sighed.

Yet, some small part of me hoped he would show up. I tried to honor what my sister said, to keep pushing, so I pushed Seven out of my mind and paid attention to the lecture. I took notes to the best of my ability. After class, I headed over to the restaurant for my shift. I was getting close to meeting enough service hours to take the exam, so I pressed through. I even took a few extra shifts just to keep my mind off of things. One evening, I called my best friend.

"Hey, Aspen, what's up?" I asked.

"Girl, you know I was getting ready to put an APB out on you since I hadn't heard from you in a few days," Aspen blew out.

"I'm sorry, just going through so much right now, but I'm cool."

"Well, that's good. I figured you were. I try not to put too much pressure on you, but you know, being way out there by yourself, I needed to hear from you. It's essential that you drop me a text or a line letting me know you're alright. I don't ask for much," Aspen said.

"I know, and I appreciate you. Liz called me, which was surprising because you know she doesn't talk on the phone."

"What did she want, some money?" Aspen joked.

"Surprisingly, she didn't ask for any money. She said she had it on her heart to call and check on me. It was crazy, too, because I was having a bit of a breakdown right before she called. I really needed to hear from somebody."

"That's good, you know. I keep telling you God never lets you go through more than you can handle. Trust me, I'm speaking from experience."

"I know. All right, well, you know it's late here, so I'm getting ready to head on to bed. I love you," I said.

"I love you too, bye.

CHAPTER
FOURTEEN

SEVEN

"Yo, when are you gonna get back on the podcast with us, man?" Monroe asked.

My boys, Charles and Monroe, took me out for some wings and beer while I was home.

"I don't know, man. You know, I got stuff popping off living in Paris," I bragged.

"Yeah, your mom told me you were gone one day when I went by there looking for you. You just left without saying anything," Monroe smirked.

"Dude, you're a whole lie. You forgot you gave me a going away party, huh," I laughed, sipping my beer.

"Oh yeah, I forgot we did give you a party, didn't we?" My bad," Charles co-signed. "No, but for real, when are you going to get back on the podcast with us?"

"Well, it might be a minute, you know, since I just lost my brother. I'm not really up to all that right now, aside from me trying to figure out what I'm going to do. You know, I wanted to buy that vineyard, but now my thoughts are to take over the family book-store so my parents can retire." I sighed.

"I mean, it doesn't have to be the end all be all," Monroe said. "Why can't you do both? Why can't you hire somebody to work at the bookstore while you get the vineyard together?"

"I don't know. I guess I never thought about it like that," I admitted.

"Man, never let life get you down. You just gotta turn things to work in your favor," Charles said.

"Yeah, I guess it's something to think about anyway," I noted.

"So, how long are you going to be in town?" Monroe asked.

"Well, I was planning not to go back, but

it seems mom really wants me to complete the exam and get my certification," I shrugged.

"What do they say, mother knows best? She obviously knows that you're going to be able to put that to use in some kind of way," Monroe pointed out.

I nodded. "Yeah, probably," I agreed.

I zoned out momentarily while those two talked about their next topic for the podcast. A lot of things had been hitting me mentally, giving me a lot to think about. I sipped my beer as I contemplated.

As the night ended, we slapped hands and said our goodbyes, going our separate ways.

They gave me a lot to think about. I had gone too far not to take that test, so when I got home, I booked flight arrangements back to Paris. Still, in the back of my mind, I couldn't figure out why I would waste time doing this when I knew I was gonna end up running that bookstore.

On the plane, I studied hard, trying to get my mind back in the game. When I returned to Paris, it was a class day. I stopped by my place, dropped off my luggage, and grabbed the things I needed for class. I headed over to the university. I was a few minutes late. Still, I went ahead inside to sit down.

Kane looked at me, but there was no spark in her eye, not the spark that I was used to seeing. I felt kind of bad about it, too, but I pulled my paper and pencil out, proceeding to take notes. After class, I thought Kane and I would talk. But by the time I grabbed my stuff and headed out, she was gone.

I was tired anyway from the flight, so I went back to my place to lay down. After another whole day had gone by, I hadn't heard from her. I hesitated to call. Hell, I was a coward at that point. I knew I had let her down after I said over and over again that I had her back.

But it wasn't too late. We hadn't taken an exam yet, I reasoned. We could jump back into our studies the way we used to. Still, my pride wouldn't let me call.

The next day I'd had enough. I headed over to the restaurant to see if Kane was working. When I got there, she was having dinner with someone. It totally surprised me.

Here I was torturing myself over her, and she had moved on with her life. I noticed she glanced my way, catching me looking at her before I turned around and walked out the door.

CHAPTER
FIFTEEN

KANE

I was sitting at the table with Andrew eating dinner. Emily had taken the girls to the restroom.

"Thank you so much for inviting me to dinner to meet your wife and kids" I said. "You have a beautiful family."

"I talk about you all the time, so Emily was just as excited to meet you. So were the girls. I told them I had a friend from the US. They really wanted to meet you because we want to plan a trip over there. I figured you could give us some good information on what to do, where to go, and what to see," Andrew pushed his glasses up on his nose.

"Of course, I would love to do that for you guys. Just let me know when you're ready."

I happened to look over to see Seven looking in my direction. I thought he was going to come inside, but for some reason, he turned around. Walking right back out the door.

I didn't understand why at first, but then I realized I was sitting there with Andrew. It appeared to be him and me since Emily, and the girls stepped away. My heart dipped.

It was crazy, though. I knew he'd been back for a couple of days, but he hadn't reached out to me at all. I was giving him space since I knew he had just buried his brother. I was trying to find my own way, honestly.

When Emily and the girls came back to the table, we got up to part ways. They had already cleaned the table, and we'd paid our bill. I was keeping him company until they came back.

"Emily, it was so good to meet you," I told her.

"For me, too," she sang.

"You guys have a great evening. Bye, girls," I said, giving them a wave.

"We'll talk again soon," she said.

"I'll see you next week, Andrew. I'm actually off for a couple of days. I'm going to use some time to study. I'm getting closer to fulfilling my service hours so I can take this exam," I smiled.

"All right, enjoy your long weekend." Andrew grabbed his daughter's hands, heading towards the door. I left the restaurant with my to-go bag in hand, stepping in long strides. I knew I missed Seven, but I hadn't realized how much I had missed him until I saw him.

Inside, I took a hot shower. Immediately climbing into bed. I wasn't in the mood to talk to anybody.

I was stuck in a bad nightmare. I didn't understand why because the dream started out so good. How had a ride on the merry-go-round with the cute little horses turned into the roller coaster from hell? I wondered. Normally I'd be up cleaning, but today I had no ambition, no push, no drive to get out of bed. So, I lay there noticing how the sun started on one side of the room and ended up on the other side. It was evening.

Finally, I did decide to get up to take a hot shower. When I got out, someone was knocking on my door. I hurried up, throwing on sweatpants and a T-shirt before wrapping a towel around my wet head. I headed to the door.

"Who is it?" I called out.

"Kane, it's Seven." My heart lurched out of my chest, happy and mad simultaneously. I opened the door.

"What do you want?" I asked. He looked at me as if he were surprised, I greeted him in that fashion. However, I did move over so he could come inside.

"You didn't waste any time moving on, did you?" He spat.

I smirked. This was going to be short and sweet.

"Listen, Seven, I'm not in the business of breaking up and making up with anybody. I came out here with goals. I admit I got off track a bit. I thought we were falling for each other. Still, I never imagined the one time that you tell me you love me would be the same time you're breaking up with me.

I shrank from the embarrassment of rejection. "I don't understand why you're coming at me this way. Oh, and for your information, I was having dinner with a coworker, his wife, and kids. Who happened to be in the restroom at the moment you assumed I was on a date."

I threw my hands up on my hips in disgust. "Imagine the irony of that," I shook my head.

"I thought we could talk." There was melancholy on his face.

"How is it talking when you immediately throw accusations at me?" I asked.

"I don't know what you expect from me. I just lost my brother. There are days when I don't know if I'm coming or going."

"Yeah, well, we could've talked weeks ago when you left that letter on my table. You could've called. You could've texted. You could've dropped a line. You could've checked to see if I was okay," I huffed.

"You severed ties with me, remember? I never expected you to do more than you could. I never asked anything of you. You were the one who kept volunteering to have my back," I cried.

"Kane—"

"No, you were the one who came into my life. I'm sorry. I don't know how to love. I am obviously broken and unworthy. And if you don't mind, I don't want to do this anymore. I wish you the best of luck, Seven. I'm so sorry that you lost your brother, but I can't do this with you. I really just want to be alone right now."

Seven stood there for several seconds like he wanted to say something, like he wanted to apologize, like he wanted to wrap his arms around me. But he didn't. He turned, moving towards the door, exactly what I expected him to do. He twisted the knob and walked out.

I picked up the nearest wine glass, hurling it at the door.

CHAPTER
SIXTEEN

SEVEN

I'm an idiot.

I had no idea why I went for Kane's juggler the way I did. She was right. I was the one who started the fight. I was the one who left her the letter, breaking things off weeks ago. I was an idiot. I don't understand why because she was the sweetest, most compassionate person I'd ever met.

I walked out her door and got in my car, driving until I didn't even know where I was any longer. I thought about how I kept telling her I had her back, yet when it came down to it, I dropped her like a hot potato. She had every right to be mad at me.

I thought about what my mom said. She told me to think about my own words. I remembered how I spoke about holding grudges and festering in that bad energy. So, why was I doing the same thing I had spoken about?

I knew my brother wanted me to take the family store. I held a grudge that he had passed away and left me to that task when I really wanted to do something else. But I also wanted to honor my brother's wish even though my mom was telling me I didn't have to. This was a tough decision to make. On top of that, I hurt the only woman I ever told I loved. My heart hurt so badly right now. Kane didn't want anything to do with me.

All I could think about was the time we spent together. The way she laid her hands on top of mine when I was hurting, how she cradled herself over my back when I found out about my brother. I could remember the twinkle in her eye when I took her to the vineyard. That made me smile.

Kane had nothing but love for me. Still, I treated her so coldly. I didn't know how to fix things. The only thing I could do was take the test and go back home to figure things out there.

Turning on the GPS to find my way back home, I eventually arrived. I went inside and poured myself a glass of wine. It sucked to be in Paris and not be with the one I loved.

I sat down, turning on the TV, but I couldn't get into anything I watched. I called my mother.

"Mom, I think I'm gonna come home. I messed up with Kane. I really don't have it in me to take the exam anymore. I'm sad about Rye. I pushed Kane away. Nothing even matters anymore." I shook my head. "I mean, I could always come back and take the test later on if I feel it'll be useful in some way," I reasoned.

"Seven, you need to figure out how to make up with Kane. She's a nice girl who took time out of her schedule to travel all the way here with you. I don't know what you did to push her away, but that girl has a head on her shoulders, not to mention she's really trying to do something with herself, unlike your last girlfriend who does nothing but run around here sleeping with all the men in town," mom noted.

"Oh, my goodness, mom, did you have to bring up Kimberlee again?" I asked.

"I'm just saying that was the worst girl you ever dated. When you brought Kane here, I saw how nice and respectful she was. The girl is smart. She's got a head on her shoulders. Her friend was so nice and respectful, too. I mean, those women are classy."

I laughed. "I know, mom, but I messed up. She doesn't even wanna talk to me anymore."

"Don't you think it would be great if you learned from your own lesson? From the words you spoke at Rye's funeral?" She asked. "Or were you just spitting words?"

"No, ma'am, I really felt that way."

"Well then, you know what you gotta do," she said.

"Thank you, mom, for listening to me. I guess I should probably lay down and get some rest."

"Alright, well, you know I love you, son. Take care, do the right thing, get yourself together," she said.

"I love you too," I told her, holding the cell phone in my hand.

CHAPTER
SEVENTEEN

KANE

"Don't be so hard on him, Kane. Do you remember when I lost my grandmother? It was months before I felt normal. I was testy anytime anybody said something to me. I was ready to pick fights over stupid stuff."

"Yeah, now that you mention it, I do remember. That was a rough time," I agreed.

"That's what I'm saying. You already told me that Seven said he and his brother were really close. They were like best friends. Can you imagine losing your best friend? Could you imagine losing me and then trying to just live like normal as if nothing happened?" Aspen asked.

"When you put it like that, no, I couldn't imagine losing you, my best friend." I smiled. "No, but seriously that's got to be awful, or even if I lost my baby sister, I don't know if I would ever be right," I confirmed.

"Exactly, so cut him some slack. Hell, he was trying to make up with your ass, saw you out to dinner with another man, and got a little jealous. Girl, you should probably worry if he didn't get jealous," Aspen laughed.

I nodded. "I guess you're right. Tomorrow's a class day. When I see him, I'll talk to him."

"Why wait till tomorrow? Just call his ass?" Aspen blew out.

"Because it's getting late," I said.

"Whatever, go on to bed, go to class tomorrow, and talk to that man."

"I already told you I would. Next week is the big exam. Then this will be over. I am ecstatic.

"I know you are. All right. Love you, girl," she said.

"Love you too, bye.

The next day I got up. I was in better spirits. I headed over to the University for class. I went in all pumped up, anxious to talk to Seven; however, he never showed up. I mean, that really scared me because he never missed class unless he was gone back home.

I was so mean to him the other day that maybe he decided to go back. That really broke my heart when I thought about it. I can't even remember the last time I'd been mean to somebody. Even when Kelley was nasty to me, I never said anything out of pocket back to her. That just wasn't my style. So, for me to have kicked him out of my place, I felt really bad about it now.

I tried my hardest to listen to the lecture. It was getting too close to the exam for me not to be paying attention, but it was hard. I couldn't imagine where he was and if he was alright. It just really ripped me up inside.

I was able to focus for a few minutes. The teacher talked about everything we'd gone over, kind of giving a recap because next week was the big exam. It was a refresher class that went on a little long.

I was disappointed that Seven had come all the way back to Paris only to miss the most important class. Afterwards, I headed over to the restaurant. I had one last shift, and then I had the rest of the week to study.

I headed inside. I tried my hardest to focus on getting through the evening. I went back to the kitchen, and the crew yelled, "Surprise."

"What is this?" I smiled.

"Congratulations, you made it to your last shift. You are free to take the test. That's an exciting moment for you," Andrew complimented.

"Congratulations," Fred, the chef, said.

"Oh my gosh, thank you, guys," I blushed.

"We have cake and wine," Fred told me.

"Yay, thank you, guys, again. This means so much to me. It's hard being way over here away from my family. So, to know you guys thought this much of me really makes me happy." I hugged all of my coworkers, and that made me smile. It made it a lot easier to get through the evening.

Later at home, I texted Seven's phone. I told him I tried to take good notes and recorded some of the lecture if he needed help.

I got no answer, even though I was concerned. I didn't feel like talking on the phone this evening. I climbed into bed, anxious for sleep to come. Sometime during the night, I must've fallen asleep and didn't realize it. I was awoken by the doorbell. I climbed out a bit curious as to who would be knocking on my door so early. It was Seven. I leaned on the door giving him a smile.

CHAPTER
EIGHTEEN

SEVEN

My shoulders drooped when she didn't answer the door at first. But then she stood there in the door jamb smiling at me.

"I'm smiling because I'm happy you're alright, but I'm still mad at you." She shifted on her legs and looked away.

"Kane." She looked in my direction at the sound of my voice but still frowned.

"What's wrong?" I asked when I noticed tears forming in her eyes. "Can I come in?"

"Yes," she said in a low whisper. "I'm crying because I was worried about you. I realized how much of a jerk I've been." Kane moved to shut the door. "I thought maybe you went back to the states."

I reached for her hand. She lifted her eyes to meet mine.

"In that letter, you said you loved me," she eased away from me. "But you pushed me away without giving me the benefit of the doubt, without any warning."

"It's true. I'm so sorry for all of that. I thought maybe it was too soon to feel the way I did about you. I wanted to make sure I wasn't vulnerable because of losing my brother. I don't know." I moved closer to her, grabbing her hand again.

I pulled Kane into my arms.

"I'm sorry. I never meant to hurt you," I told her. "I've honestly been a little crazy since my brother passed. I've never dealt with this kind of pain before."

Kane whispered. "I know," I'm sorry for not understanding and not being more sup-portive. It wasn't the right time to be worried about the test because, honestly, I would walk away from this right now if you needed me to," she cried.

I used my thumbs to brush the tears off her cheeks before pressing my lips to hers.

"I love you."

Kane cupped my face. "I love you, too."

"I told you I had your back which is why I'm right here. We gotta hit these books. A little birdy told me you had the answers," I laughed, ducking a swat from Kane.

"Come on, I need coffee first," she smiled.

"Get dressed. I would like to take a ride on the train into the city and have lunch. We can catch up since we haven't talked in a while. Then we can come back and study. How does that sound?" I asked.

"I would love to do that. I think I can spare one afternoon," Kane replied.

Once Kane was dressed, we headed outside. "Hold on, I got to get something out of my car," I told her.

I ran over to my car and opened the trunk. I could've driven, but I thought it would be more romantic to ride the train. I grabbed a duffel bag out of the back, heading back in Kane's direction.

"What are you doing with that huge bag? Are you going to carry that?" She questioned.

"Yeah, it's not heavy. I didn't want to leave it in the car. It's just some chairs for us to sit on in case we decide to go to the park or something."

"That's weird because we always sit on the bench in the park," she frowned.

"Just roll with it," I answered, not knowing what else to say.

We walked two blocks over to the main street, where we caught the train. Once we got on, I got busy. I pulled out a small fold-up table and sat it in front of us. Then I put a white tablecloth over it. Pulled out a bottle of wine. I placed the wine on the table and pulled out a little vase with the flower bud stuck inside.

"What are you doing?" Kane squealed as people on the train started pointing and smiling at us. I pulled two wine glasses out of the bag and set them on the table. Then I opened the wine pouring two glasses.

Kane looked around, blushing. She was so embarrassed. I mean, I literally did pull a whole table out on the train.

Next, I dug down in my bag and pulled out the maraschino cherries, dropping one in each glass. She looked away as if she didn't know me. But then I picked up my wine glass. She gave in and grabbed her flute.

"Cheers," I said, clinking my glass against hers.

Once more, I dug down in the bag and pulled out a platter with a silver dome over it, setting it on the table.

"I hope you're hungry," I smiled.

"Oh, my goodness. So, we're just gonna eat with all of these people looking at us?" Kane asked between gritted teeth.

"Yes."

I continued to lay out the spread.

"Go on, lift the lid and eat. I know you're hungry."

Kane lifted the lid, exposing a black velvet ring box underneath.

"Oh my God, no, you didn't!" She cried.

I picked up the ring box and moved around the table in front of her. I got down on one knee.

"Kane Amore, will you marry me?" I asked.

Kane lifted her eyebrows as she threw her hand over her mouth.

"Girl, you better tell that man yes," some woman on the train hollered.

My eyes went wide with anticipation of her answer.

"Yes, yes, I will marry you."

I pulled Kane up from her seat, where we hugged and kissed right there on the train in front of everyone.

"I love you so much," she said.

"I love you, too.

CHAPTER
NINETEEN

KANE

My lips parted in surprise when I opened my exam results. It said I had passed. A big smile spread across my lips.

"Your turn," I said to Seven as he held the manila envelope with his name typed on the front.

Seven pulled the piece of paper out of the envelope, his brows furrowed together.

"What is it?" I asked, worried.

But then a smile spread across his mouth. I slapped his arm.

"Damn, you scared me."

Seven swept me off my feet as we celebrated.

"Do you realize you just made history, becoming the first master sommelier with dyslexia?" He asked.

"Wow," I hadn't thought about it like that. "You know, I don't think I want to claim that anymore. Like I'll still advocate and help others, but I want my story to be about how I overcame a learning disability," I smiled.

"That's great. I love that for you," Seven told me.

"Now, we can start building our lives," I said.

"Yes, let's pack. We're going home," Seven stuffed his certificate back inside his envelope and moved to the computer to book our flights.

We spent the next couple of days cleaning out our apartments, turning in keys, and saying goodbye to our friends. On the way to turn in Seven's leased car, we went over to The Pond des Arts, the famous Lock Bridge, and added our padlock to its railing. Then we threw the key into the river below.

"Can you believe we got engaged in Paris?" I asked on our flight to Oakland.

"No, I had no idea I would leave Paris with the love of my life," Seven smiled at me. We laced fingers before nodding off to sleep. Fifteen hours later, we arrived in Oakland and drove to Napa Valley.

We arrived to a welcome home dinner celebration Mrs. Smith put together to introduce me to some of the other family members.

Everyone wanted us to show off our sommelier skills, asking about different wines. We also had to give a full account of how he proposed to me on the train. Luckily, he was able to record it by propping his phone on the table without my knowledge.

I looked around at his family, grateful for whatever was next.

A few days later, his mother decided it was time for the reading of Rye's will. We gathered around the table as the attorney opened his briefcase. The scene was bittersweet, causing me to squeeze Seven's hand in assurance.

I honestly zoned out, not wanting to listen to all the technicalities. However, the reading was short, sweet, and to the point. Rye had left Seven enough money to purchase the vineyard and then some.

Seven hugged his parents and then me. The attorney gave Seven a piece of paper to sign and handed him a certified check before closing his briefcase. Mr. Smith walked him to the door.

"I have an idea. I don't know how you'll feel about it but what if you build a new bookstore on the vineyard where people can drink wine and buy books at the same time?" I suggested.

"I like that idea, and my parents can still retire, leaving their legacy behind," he said.

"I would love that so much, a wine bookstore," his mother smiled. "I don't know. You're likely to find me inside daily reading a book with a glass of wine, too." We laughed.

"Hey babe, I'm going to head to bed," I said to Seven.

He squeezed my hand. "I'll be back in a few."

When I reached our room, I dialed Aspen's number.

"I'm back," I squealed.

"I'm so glad. I missed you so much." Aspen laughed. "I knew you were going to go over there and get you a big tall tree."

"Aspen, you are a fool. Yes, I went to Paris and found the love of my life."

THE END

Enjoy the story? Please be sure to leave a review!

Also by Amber Ghe

Reading Order

Dear Readers,

All of my series can be read independently of one another. However, most of them are connected, and if you read the series in the order, I wrote them, you'll discover more depth to the stories and characters. Some of your favorite characters make appearances in later series, so if you'd like to glean the greatest depth from my writing, here's my suggested reading order.

The Mergers & Acquisitions Series:

Mergers & Acquisitions (Book 1)

Game Faces On (Book 2)

Dreams Under Construction (Book 3)

The Dream Series: Can be read as standalone - spinoff characters from Mergers & Acquisitions (Book 1)

To Steal a Dream (Standalone)

Christmas Chance (Standalone)

Wait for Tonight (Standalone)

Mixfits Series: Conspiracy Series

Mixfits (Book 1)

Mixfits (Book 2)

The Sins of OG (Standalone)

Bliss Way Short Stories: Books have a common theme; they are all single parents and live on Bliss Way – not connected.

Bliss Way

Candid for You

Love Makes Scents (free)

The Billionaire Bae Series:

Family First (free)

Honor (Book 1)

Valor (Book 2)

Power(Book 3)

Spirit (Book 4) Coming Soon

ABOUT THE AUTHOR

Amber Ghe is the author of the compelling 'Billionaire Bae' series, penning romance stories with a hint of sizzle and women's fiction. She writes about characters who examine their lives, hopes, fears, and motivations, characters that will linger with you long after the story is over. She dreams that the Billionaire Bae series will become an internet series or motion picture one day.

She's made it her mission to encourage healthy self-esteem, attitude, and woman empowerment. While practicing her daily mantra, Girl, 'Show up for Your Life!' she's decided to make that her movement. A jack of all trades, she loves to dabble in art, design, movies, and of course, reading.

Working a nine-to-five by day and author by night, she hopes to make it a full-time job one day. She currently resides in Ohio with her husband, where she is a full-time mom.

She's following her real passion by working on her subsequent novels.: Connect on social media

- f facebook.com/authoramberghe
- instagram.com/author_amber_ghe_new
- tiktok.com/@author_amber_ghe
- twitter.com/Author_AmberGhe